Blue Dog, Green River

BLUE DOG,
GREEN RIVER

a novel by BROCK BROWER

illustrated by NANCY LAWTON

DAVID R. GODINE · *Publisher*

BOSTON

First published in 2005 by
David R. Godine, Publisher
Post Office Box 450
Jaffrey, New Hampshire 03452
www.godine.com

LIBRARY OF CONGRESS
CATALOGING-IN-PUBLICATION DATA

Brower, Brock, 1931-
Blue Dog, Green River : a novel / by Brock Brower ;
illustrated by Nancy Lawton.— 1st ed.
p.   cm.
ISBN 1-56792-280-5 (Hardcover : alk. paper)
1. Dogs—Fiction. 2. Dog owners—Fiction.
3. Human-animal relationships—Fiction.
4. Green River (Wyo.-Utah)—Fiction.
I. Lawton, Nancy. II. Title.
PS3552.R683B58   2005
813'.54—dc22
2004016528

First Edition
PRINTED IN THE UNITED STATES OF AMERICA

To Ann, again

"I spaced the dog."

Paul Nozik started telling me this story up on a rough Navajo sandstone ledge that butted out over Flat Iron Rapid. We'd pulled our kayaks onto a wet spit of sand, maybe two hundred yards back along the green gaggle of the shoreline. Paul knew every eddy gate you could tuck into along this canyon stretch of the Green, running deep down a mile and back out again, straight through Deso. We'd come up to scout the rapid, the water still pretty high for late June. Frothy current arrowed through ducts in the flat slice of sandstone, spitting like steam off a hot iron. I was ready to try her, but Paul wanted to have a sit.

"Just plain spaced Blue Dog. Part account of I had this four-day party of L.A. strummers and twangers and tootlers and pounders to float through Deso, down to Roof Rock and out. Some of them liked to tootle over the rapids. Not country or anything you hear regular. They play pure classical. Like you get on the car radio, off those low numbers way up the front end of the dial?

"I had ten of them, altogether. Two year ago, they were only a trio. One big, one little fiddler, and a pipe

7

guy. Then Bob Hoskins, the big fiddler, got himself a redhead who saws away at this cello atween her knees. More a cow fiddle than a bull fiddle. They're a foursome now, the Green River Quartet. They love to play under the ledges for the echoes. That's why Roof Rock. This summer they went big band, formed a group, what Hoskins' girl Larry wrote me was going to be a chamber orchestra. I got to calling them the Green River Chamber Pots, and it took.

"I'm the first day out with these Chamber Pots, 'nough of a job keeping their instruments tied down in the rafts. But I got one tootler keeps pulling out his oboe. This weirdo thing like a clarinet? Got the same long barrel with the same holes and clamps all up and down it, but this squiggly little jigger up top? Like a twisted straw he kept sucking on. Or blowing through. This tootler, Mike something, says he is playing us water music. My chief boatman Russ is Marin County, strapping big blond, but educated Yale, knows more music than I do. 'That's Handel,' he tells me, says it's like what you take hold of something by. Made the most godawful weasel-whistle sounds. Drove Blue Dog damn crazy. Her ears can't take it.

"You seen how she rides the raft, up on the stern pillow? The wind keeps her dry, stirs her curls up good, like fresh tar in wood shavings. She likes to sniff at the breezes. All that bounce the raft gives you, she takes on a four-legged crouch. That's the sheepdog in her. But she'll dive off and swim alongside, some-

8

times, and that's the Lab in her. Big furry web feet, like matched hairbrushes, fore and aft. I seen her swim through most any rapid. Dive under too, got to be some Newfy, even bloodhound in her. Done that to get away from the tootling, afore I swung us into Cat Lick for lunch.

"Then I didn't see her, figgered she must already slipped ashore, gone after varmints. I got my mind on how am I gonna move all their instruments safe ashore at Roof Rock? Including a harp. I kid you not. They got it boxed up in this big black case, but that only makes it one size bigger all around. The guy they got playing the harp is an albino. Dead white hair, and when you look close, pink eyes. Forget his name, we just called him Al. He was a sight, plucking on those strings in the moonlight, grinning like some werewolf, clawing all the high notes on that last little lick of short strings, up by his ear, but I'll get to that.

"You seen Roof Rock, maybe five miles back. Big, wide, natural amphitheater – hollowed out like a giant bat cave, with this booming echo. But they never had no audience. They come just to hear what they sound like to themselves. The rocks roll the music right back over top of them, like the surge off a waterfall. I've heard it sound huge."

Paul had on his yellowdog sunglasses that mirror back at you, like a Dallas bank building. Those, and his fierce red beard, make him a menace down on the river, hunkered into his red kayak, paddling smooth but ferocious, like some sleek aquatic centaur. Half man, half boat. But here he was, with his rubber spray skirt hanging loose, fetched up behind his own two naked, red-hairy legs, hugging them for moral support.

"Anyways, I hauled out that one-man neoprene raft I been keeping back, all collapsed, I still got from World War Two Surplus. It's so ripped full of holes from tearing over these river rocks, might of gone ashore at Tarawa, could of been at Midway. I was always saying I'm gonna repair the bottom, glue up the holes so this time I can pump enough air into her to use her for a dory. I got three rafts to unload, with help from Russ up in the lead raft, then Pam boating the middle raft, who can't tote that much. And there are more instruments than Chamber Pots when it's gonna come time to run that cello and the flugelhorns and fiddles and the damn harp, over those razors in front of Rock Roof.

"I leave Russ and Pam to chow them down while I struggle to get this rubber duckie afloat out on the string I'm running downriver that afternoon. I must of done a dozen patches, like big black corn plasters. When Russ has them fed and set to go, I give the neoprene a few pumps with the foot bellows, and the first hint of pressure, blew-y! It's a kamikaze. Forget it, says Russ, we got to move. So it's gonna be a ship-to-shore hand-off, if we can get there before moonrise."

Paul hugged his legs and scrunched a full foot forward on the sandstone, hard on his buttocks, then waved across at the dusky canyon walls.

"You get to thinking all this looks like some Valley of the Moon, mountains to the left of you, peaks to the right of you. But where you are, really, at this moment on earth, is a long ways down a big crack. How much light do you ever get down any crack? We're herding these Chamber Pots into the three rafts, and all I can think is, how we gonna make time? And all we got is the same damn rolling river current that began trickling in from Wyoming when winter broke, three months ago, less what the goddamn dam is holding back on us.

"And that's when I spaced Blue Dog.

"Never missed her, all the way to Rock Roof. Thought she must be up with Russ in the lead raft, or swimming along the side somewhere, barking at the catfish. Only how come I don't hear her watery bark? Pretty distinct, when you stop to think she's both barking and swimming at the same time in a running current. And why ain't she popped up on the stern pillow, grabbing a wet-claw hold like some boarding black pirate until I reach out and give her a haul aboard, like I always do?

"I begin to worry, but I can't go back. Never mind that water only flows one way, I've got to push this load with their calliope and all into Roof Rock, then I got another party of Knols kids farther downstream at the Ghost Ranch. I'm supposed to check them out, come Wednesday, and fly out with the plane Thursday morning. This Piper one-lung that Jeff Harrington operates off the mesa over Moab, hops in and out of the canyon like a right slick grasshopper, but you got to be there when it jumps.

"I'm thinking hard, Blue Dog never done this afore. Or better, I never spaced her like this. I had her over a year, took her from the pound in Moab. She was savage then, a real bad mix and gimpy. So much a mix that she has those two-color eyes. Brown to port, blue to starboard. I named her Blue Dog for the way she cocks her head, goes starboard watch. She's got a long gaze in that blue eye.

"But she's gimpy because she got shot. Buckshot, nasty. In the left hinder, from stealing chickens. She's a well-known chicken thief around Moab, so cagey that she don't ever bark. Only a little bit of growl, back in her throat. When you're on the prowl, why give away your whereabouts? But that means to me smart, and that's why I took her, day afore they were gonna put her down. We got this Stunt Man's Museum in Moab? I figgered her for the stunt man's dog. Wound wasn't healed yet. Soon as it did, I dropped her off the raft, into the river. I seen the Lab and the Newfy in her. It was quit chickens or drown, she had to make a swift choice.

"I figgered if I soaked her good, and long enough, she'd go straight. Knew she was gonna be all right when she started barking again. At the catfish and the carp, but didn't go for them. Same way she'll bark at the Utes' scrub cattle if they wander down too near our campsites. It was just sort of joyful. Didn't growl at anything but maybe a scorpion.

"But she always stuck with the raft. Where'd she got to? Could she make it on her own, out there, or back there, or where-to-hell-ever she was gone to? Was she strong enough to be out on her lonesome, in Deso?

"Desolation Canyon. John Wesley Powell named it right. And I can show you where he got hisself cliffed, though some say that was back in Lodore. Had to haul him up out of big trouble by someone else's long johns.

"But what could I do? Wait it out, send word back upstream to grab her, tie her up, I'd come a-running, soon as I could. I remembered Marv Carter had a party going into Cat Lick that night, and whoever Marv had boating would know Blue Dog if she was still hanging there, would know what to do with her, how to treat her right.

"What I didn't know was what kind of a party Marvin had on his hands. He had the same bunch last year, out of Denver, swore he wasn't gonna take them again, they were so drunk rowdy. But then he figgered the bucks, if he stuffed all these no-goods in that big silver-shiner balsam barge he's got. He could cut them loose with his Jap boatman, we call him Thai Chee, and forget about them until they washed out of Deso. You can't even fall overboard drunk out of that shiner barge, hard as these trash were sure to try. You're safe cargo.

"But they were a mean lot, the dregs of whatever

never made it over the Rockies. Remember those traffic controllers went on strike, back in '80, and Reagan
fired all their asses? Never got their jobs back, and some
of them ended up working on the Denver garbage
trucks. That's them. They were real bitter angry at life,
and brought along enough women to take it out on. As
hard luck as they come. And harder luck they ever
crossed with Blue Dog."

Swimming hard, with her black snout up on pilot, the dog made for shore. She could smell its green heat. Her front paws dug early into clinging sand, churning up a fog cloud of silt, before she legged into a splashy sprint toward the dry strand. Once out of the ripple, she set all four feet and shook herself like a small, dark thunderhead, throwing squalls and a quick rainbow. Then she scuttled into the green rushes.

She left those still coming ashore to drag and lug and hustle, set on her own hunting. She wove through hot red rocks and troughs of baking greenery, and her nose kept her skittering after every stray scent. She caught the pungency of some rock critter, lost it weaving through a murk of cow flop, then tweaked on the sudden stink of a very close evil.

She crouched, facing a flat table of sandstone, on which lay coiled two feet of what looked like rope. The rope was rose colored, but tied into darker, diamond-shaped knots. It did not move when the dog made a sand-kicking feint from her crouch, but a whir came out of its neat coils.

She didn't much care for that stink on the rock, but

knew better than to go for it, yank at it. She did a couple more feints on her fast front paws, but it still did not budge. The whir ticked again. From long past, a low growl rose in her throat, answering the whir. She poked her wet nose nearer the stink, then jutted her muzzle, snarling through bared teeth.

The rope went stiff, lifted and whipped out. That end frayed open.

The dog dodged back from the fraying. The rope whipped around into a rosy ess, writhing inside its knots. Another whipping action snapped the frayed end, but it missed her muzzle again – just – and she retreated to her haunches.

The rope started to slip off the rock.

She bobbed her head to watch with her blue eye. When it was far enough over the edge, dropping onto the sand, but too loose to coil, she pounced.

She sank her teeth into it, at an almost middle knot, but the frayed end got her this time. She yelped at the drilling sting, had to let go, and thrust her muzzle into the agony in her left hind leg, the gimpy one.

The rope took a big twist, essing to slip under the rock. But it was broke-bent at the middle knot, and couldn't finish its sweeping curve.

She stopped nuzzling the wound, kicked back spastically with her struck leg, then shifted around toward the flailing rope.

It was whirring, ready to whip again. But she saw that all she had to do was get behind it.

She circled, growling and kicking sand. She feinted at it, then leapt back as quickly, if it half whipped at her. When she had it feebly twisted around backwards, she hunkered down, snuffling her snout into the sand. Then she sprang, scooped with her lower jaw, and crunched through its last writhing jiggery.

It hung from her muzzle like limp shag.

She shook both tag ends with the heft of her jaws, almost in mockery, and headed back toward the river with her prize.

But the rafts were already afloat, out in the green current, running away from her.

She hopped into the water, as deep as she could go without swimming. She wanted to bark but couldn't let go what dangled from her muzzle. She leapt up on her hind legs, splashing, driven to plunge after them, still with her prey. But after a few attempts, she saw they were too far gone and struggled back to shore.

There she stood starboard watch while the rafts slipped, like huge lilypads, over the river's falling edge.

At this last, she dropped the rope onto the sand and lay down herself, pointing her black muzzle, like a blunt compass, toward the quadrant where they had vanished. Instinct told her to keep patient guard, to wait for them to return, but it was blind instinct that knew no span of days, no vista but the darkening river that must somehow bring them back round.

Then they seemed to be coming again. Late in the

day, but from upriver, in a big silvery barge trolling through the sinking sun's last fiery ripples. The barge crossed the great rose sunset glow on the canyon walls like a floating bowl, alive with lifted arms and rude shouts and loud laughter. But she saw there would be no arm to reach for her, haul her over its silver sides into safety and comfort. From this far away, she could see they had no mastery over others, nor themselves.

They flopped ashore from the barge, some of them dragging what looked like a small dredge up the sand.

"Beer, beer, beer! We're here, here, here with the beer, beer, beer!"

They yanked colorful cans out of the dredge, tossed them to each other, then emptied them down their throats, or shook them up and streamed frothy jets at each other. Two women in wet jeans and drenched T-shirts ran away from this sudsy deluge, almost into the dog.

"Hey, we got us a hound dog!"

"Shit. He got a snake."

They ran back again, almost into the Japanese boatman, who was trying to jostle the party into getting their gear ashore before nightfall.

"Jimminee!" he said, but looked carefully. "That snake's good as dead." He tossed the tents toward the two women. Then he reached down to pet the dog's muzzle. "This here's Paul Nozik's raft dog."

He rubbed the dog's head behind her ears, and

turned toward his party, silently inviting them to do the same, but their attention was bleary, elsewhere.

The women were looking to the men to put up the tents, and the men were already too busy drinking to put up anything.

"Thai Cheese," one of them yelled. "You didn't tell us you got snakes."

"Only a little canyon rattler," the boatman said. "Got no venom, not much rattle. You get stung worse by scorpions, so better kick up the sand" – he tried hinting at work still to do – "before you roll out your bedding."

But the party was already on. They were roaring out drinking songs that ended in commands to chug-a-lug, like the clunking of railroad tracks.

"What you doing here, Blue Dog?" the boatman whispered. "Don't I got enough grief?"

"Get us shut of that snake!" one of them yelled.

Rather than argue, Thai Chee took his boat pole, lifted the dead snake, and hove it into the rushes. The dog turned her brown eye on him, like a soft cry, then got up off her sandy belly and slipped away into the rushes. She was favoring her left hind leg badly.

"And don't bring it back!" the boatman whispered. And why on earth was Paul Nozik letting his dog loose again like some junkyard stray?

He rustled up the cooking fire and laid the wirework grill while his party were still fumbling with their tents. If you ladies don't lend a hand here, one of the gents snarled, no telling who you're gonna have to sleep with. The two women didn't see how that made no never-mind, they were worse worried about the mosquitos.

By then, the boatman had the oil hot in the frypan and was unwrapping chicken parts. One of the men, rapidly turning into the ugliest of the drunks, hurled a spent beer can. Maybe at the fire, maybe at him.

"You make that all chicken and no snake, Thai Cheese," he belched. "Or I'm gonna fry you up a piece of your own little yella snake."

"I shake each piece," the boatman tried to joke back. "If it rattle, I don't bake."

They took that for hilarious and drank hard to that goddamn chinkaboo, always got to have one along for your cook. Grease bubbled from the chicken skins, sizzled back at them. He served them the legs and thighs and breasts on paper plates, straight from the frypan, so hot they browned the paper. One of the women burned her mouth. "What damn good are you gonna be tonight?" the ugly drunk heehawed.

The dog slunk back out of the rushes at the smell of chicken, but sat down on her haunches, well out of the firelight. She raised her nose to the scent, uneasy with hunger, but did nothing more than give a mew that wasn't a bark. She made it look almost like a yawn, not a hunger pang.

None of his party noticed her back with them again, but the boatman pressed his hand low to the ground, and she obeyed his signal, and lay down flat.

She was holding tight to the taboo against chicken, but her stomach was in slow agony.

So was her left hinder, which she chewed to stop her growing hunger.

Then the ugliest drunk reached out and pulled the frypan off the grill, still sputtering with a few leftover chicken pieces, and set it down in the sand. He wanted to play another game, burning paper plates.

"Scale them into the fire," he ordered.

The dog raised up, alert to the greasy crackle. The scent was fading, and hadn't they set aside the frypan?

The boatman lowered his hand at her again, forcefully.

But she was off her haunches, on a skulking run. She bounded to the frypan and swept her muzzle into the settling grease. She grabbed at the flesh parts with snapping jaws, sloughed up a thigh, then scurried hard away, digging so deep that she kicked sand straight into the face of the ugliest drunk.

He was up, fumbling and furious, swearing to get that "goddamn chicken-thieving mongrel bitch!"

They remembered he liked showing them that he had a gun, and when he started yanking wildly at his wading-jacket pocket, they all ducked. The girls squealed together, and the other men rolled away from him, and Thai Chee raised up his high palm, as if to stop a deadly rush of traffic.

He finally had to rip the pocket to get the gun out. The ragged tearing tangled its barrel, almost toppling

him off his unsteady feet, but left him perilously waving a weapon in his fat, slippery hand.

It was an old Smith & Wesson thirty-eight caliber, with a clump of torn threads caught on the rusty sight. He tried to pull the threads free, and yanked wrong. A crashing shot nicked the boatman's upraised hand. Thai Chee grabbed at the pain, tried to drop out of sight as the enraged man stumbled and ran right over him.

He was scrambling toward the river, taking uncertain aim over a fleeing shadow. His own shadow, scuttling before him. A shadow that plunged into the dark ahead with his grudges, his bad luck, his wasted days, the terrible downtime that still remained for him to live out. But no letting up. He was determined to lay down fire at that crazy cur, racing over the flurries of sand, breaking this way, that way, to outrun his shadow.

He fired twice at the dog on this wobbly chase to the river, then went down, fell on his knees, using both hands to squeeze off another and another water-spouting round.

Altogether, he cracked off all but one of the six chambers. The barrel spit into the hissing water, which brought both a burst of speed and a shift of cunning in that creature he saw gunneling across the river's green flats.

He still kept back one round, squinting for a last clear shot, to make sure.

"Play dead!" he shouted, drunkenly. "Play goddamn dead, you goddamn hell-hound bitch!"

"How could I of knowed what was up?" Paul shrugged. "I didn't talk to Thai till I got back out of Deso, and he come by to ask if he could hire on with me, didn't want nothing more to do with Marv Carter's pissing parties. Thai was sick enough sorry. He thought that Armed Response shithead had shot Blue Dog, left her dead and adrift somewhere out in the river roil, who could tell? 'Did you know she was snake-bit too?' I asked him. 'Jimminee,' he tells me.

"But can't blame him. I said I'd take him on. I got him up at the Ghost Ranch right now.

"Can't really blame Marv too much either. Marv's put in a few good years since he started out of Dinosaur, running through Lodore Canyon, back when we were struggling to get the Sierra Club onto the river to see what they needed to save. Marv bought that barge off of Army Surplus, same as me, and he floated folks around Steamboat Rock up in Echo Park, two dozen at a go, back in the early '50s. Also took them down there in assault boats, any distressed war merchandise that come handy, and it paid off about even, Marv says. Steamboat Rock up there like some paddlewheeler, still one grand sight. The Yampa coming in at that fork, right there at the joining with the Green, where the red rock meets up with all that white Weber sandstone, like blood and bone. I swear it looks like God's own shoulder blade, left to bleach in the sun.

"But Marv seen better days. That barge he painted silver is really a floating bridge pontoon we never did need to cross the Rhine, count of General Patton. Marv kept filling it full of what is it you call 'em now? Enviros? Dumb damn stupid name. Did we ever call 'em Sierros?

"Marv has to make his buck, same as me, and did I get paid enough for porting all those ukes and tinkly stuff into that cave at Roof Rock? You gotta realize besides that harp, they brought their fold-up music stands and their fold-up chairs.

"They took their own sweet time most of Tuesday, went exploring along the talus, or off on hikes up that side canyon, Maggie's Grotto, where you can do some pretty fair glyphing. But his girl Larry kept after Bob, so they slowly got theirselves set up for an evening concert, full moonlight. Unfolded their chairs, lined up their candles and lanterns on the wobbly stands. Two of them had miner's lamps strapped on their foreheads, so they could read the music. Didn't really have a leader, just sat down and stomped time at each other, and let loose.

"Russ and Pam and me sat ourselves on an outside rock, and Russ tells me they're starting off with Ravel,

26

which he says like when you repel off a cliff. The harp is big and slidy and scarey on this hummer. That albino claws at those wink-wink strings, like he is unravelling some big tangle, needs all the help he can get unsnarling this music. That stirs up the bats, looping in and out, fierce. They are way way up there, lofting around on the vibes, and that spook on the harp has really got blood in his eye.

"But it's pretty, I grant you. Next is Bach, Russ whispers, which he says just like the beer. Two Chamber Pots got these two little fiddles, don't fit under their chins. 'Stead, they strum them straight up atween their knees, same as that Larry girl does her cello. Gambling violins, Russ says. Anyways, one for all, all for one, straight into Bach. Amazing how a flute and a fiddle can make the same note, so close you can't tell the peep from the twang unless you really look at who is doing what. Russ tells me they're the Brandenbergs. Not much for the harp to do, sitting it out. But everybody else is set on weaving whatever he's untangled back together again.

"But how can they waste it like that, just let it tear loose, all on its lonesome, to go out into the night air?

"That's my thought, listening to the concert echoing out of Roof Rock. More folks ought to be hearing all this. The limestone hangs down in curtains, like petrified billows. That cave goes so high, your eyes get lost in the dark, looking up, 'cept for those bats circling. Anyways, I got this idea these Brandenbergs are

27

all one rush of music, running together out of this cave, and you know how I see it really works?

"The Brandenbergs are like a braided river. You got the flow rippling and running down all these channels, and they slip together, then meander off, or cut back cross stream, suck under a rock ledge, head through the willows, spin into a whirly pool, go every which way. But it is still all one current, flowing one way only, to the very last. You got to keep picking up the current, no matter how damn devious Bach has the music doing runs and eddies and rapids, or going down God knows what gollywoggle hole.

"I said to Russ you got to be just as smart in the middle of this music as a trout lying deep in the shadow of a rock, keeping to his pool. You got to *feel* the current, so keep your head upstream. It's natural for the trout, how else does it feed? But that's the way you got to lay your ears back when you're listening to the Brandenbergs. Russ nods, says there is a piece of music by somebody named like Sherbert, it's even *called* 'The Trout.'

"But Russ don't know what kind of trout. He got the fiddlers and the oboe to play a little of it for me, hoking around, before we set off the next day, and I'd say more likely a brookie than a brown. But could be a rainbow.

"Russ is joking how I'm becoming a real music lover, but sugar, I get all my thoughts from the river.

It's deep out front of Roof Rock, picking up speed, and we can see a sizable grey tree trunk floating by, like some stripped corpse in the moonlight with too many arms and legs we ought to go catch and haul out, let dry for firewood.

"So I start down after that tree skeleton. Half on the sly, sneaking off from the Brandenbergs. They are going after some pretty high-blown notes, when one of them, Jerry something, looks a lot like Lewis, stands up with this curleycue trumpet, no valves. Jerry is one nervous guy, but trumpet guys are all like that, Russ tells me. They hit one wrong note, everybody hears it, and no escape if you're up there, solo. Jerry works his lip and really spits a few. They blare out of the rock and kick off the water, 'nough to split your ear like a shard of slate.

"That's when I first hear her, over the music.

"From somewhere other side of the river, I figgered. A howl that slaps back across the water, straight at the music. She's not barking, that's the first thing I know for sure, but it is definitely Blue Dog. Not fierce or loud enough yet to break into their music, but I can feel it, straight up the back of my neck, her next howl already on the rise.

"So is she come up, out of the water, swum all this way from Cat Lick? Is she here looking for me?

"But then she'd of barked. I am already running to one of the rafts, now with Russ, both of us shouldering the pillow, scraping the bottom down the sand. We're into its rubbery air pings, and I'm unshipping the oars when that next howl come full shiver, across the water, like to curdle your blood.

"That stopped them playing. The cave all of a sudden gulped back all their sound and filled up with the howl.

"Cause that is how she sang it out. She had to be out of the river to do that, I figgered, high up on the ledges, the other shore. That howl strung out long 'nough to snag its own echo, come back up the gorge. Then she let up, and we just sat in the raft, touching the oars to keep even with the current. No sense trying to reach her if she'd already got that far down the canyon, wasn't swimming to meet us, or barking to come aboard.

"'Something's wrong,' I told Russ.

"Then she let loose that last howl. I got to say, it shook me. Shook me to the core cause I could hear the bloodhound in her, baying as ruthless woeful as a banshee. If it had been her ears hurting from the music, I'd of understood, but nothing was coming out of the cavern, only all of them sitting around, in shock and stillness.

"She was giving it out, wild. She raised that howl like a blood threat, and the coyotes picked it up, full chorus, already after her bloody leavings.

"'She's gone back,' I had to say to Russ. 'She's gone back on us.'

"And that chamber full of them sat there, not moving, stunned silent. Not the harp, not the fiddles or the flutes or the trumpet or any of them ready to risk another note that might rouse her to howl again."

An hour into the river, the dog had stopped swimming.

Savvy, not fear, had first driven her in. The crack of the pistol was too familiar. Sharp, fiery bursts from the angry past that sent her on a zigzag scurry to escape the stench of man. Man was once more the scourge against appetite, the origin of pain, but most of all, a smoking afterstink, burning in her nostrils.

She had plunged into the water, taking panicky bites at the swirling, bug-laden shimmer. Aft of her, the pistol took one more stinking bite. Equally unrewarded. Gnats stirred and clouded and hummed, thick as mist. She tugged away from shore, with a telltale wake trailing off her ruffy neck, like a floating scarf. But the gauzy wake was soon lost under moon ripples.

Danger was a drunken shout that lay behind her, but could still lurk silently ahead. She knew to be wary, either way.

She thrust her muzzle forward, and pushed all her muscular heft into breasting the river's green gulf. The river answered with its own embrace, hauled her into its heaving flow and bore her off, downstream.

Afloat, and hummocky, like a tangled cast of reeds.

She paddled hard, lugging herself toward the middle course, but her left hind leg could not keep pace with her other stroking paws. Over the long hour, river silt thickened her black fur, and she fought against an aching lethargy that seeped through her. Catfish swam as near as their whiskers, sidling up to nibble at her fur. She tried to stay straight with the current, but it kept turning her lamed hinder, dragging her downstream into its spiraling surges.

She couldn't keep up, and couldn't keep struggling. And then she just went soggy.

Headed toward the rapids banked by larkspur. The current heading her. Barely afloat, if that.

She knew how to handle rapids. When she had to, she could swim them like an otter. When she did not want to, she took them agilely from her crouch on the stern air pillow of the raft, or she jumped out early and swam for the bank before she ever reached them, then trotted on around. Once, when the raft was about to taco down the big hole at the lava-formed falls – folding over double like a tortilla stuffed with all aboard – she had leapt clear, a full ten feet straight through the rainbow spray, and landed on the only ledge to shoreward, flat hard on all fours. Then she kept on leaping, across the talus, from rock to rock, and plunged into a foaming tuck of roil that brought her out right where all the spilled people were clamped to the raft for dear life. They took heart at her bark and followed her wet fur and flagged tail to shore.

But now she was not even stroking her paws.

Ahead of her, the river arrows butted their points into the foaming horizon. The flood caught her, turned her hard around, then shoved her into the largest of the flatwater arrowheads.

She was sucked in, sent tumbling like a spent carcass.

The carcass swept down the frothing chute, legs up in the turbulence, stiff as sticks. Then the legs disappeared into a whitening roar of rocks. For half a minute, she was good as gone. But the raging rapid gave a freak grimace that twitched the carcass out of the rocks, like some gristle caught in its teeth. The carcass rolled over the last sharp-shaved stones on a cushion of water, plumped up with flow into a moving mound. Then the rapid pitched her into the shallows, where she lay slack in the sun, like that day's drowned beast.

But her rib cage was moving, barely, slowly, in and out. After a time, her feet tucked under, got her up far enough to retch a curdle of green.

Then she shakily rose to all fours.

She limped out of the purling shallows, hupped up onto dry land, and once more sniffed out the scratched path heading down canyon. From these rapids near larkspur, the path fell into a steady descent, dropping steeply, thinly, toward the mile-down low point of Deso.

A memory trace told her Down was the only way out.

She trotted along the path, keeping back from the river. Her large head was still full of underwater echoes, like a rattled conch shell, and she shook her floppy ears to clear out these menacing sounds.

Only when she ran dead up against an outcropping did she slip back into the river and swim out to steal a ride around on its unbridled current.

Her paws were soon sore, some of her pads bleeding, but she kept to the rocks, all that night.

At dawn, she crawled off the path, under some elder, and slept through to noon, cowled by buzzing flies. She had a dog dream that seized her legs, set her whimpering. She broke into a twitching run, but toward nowhere. Neither away, nor homeward – lying flat on her side, kicking up dirt with her big paws, but still limping – until the dream came to a sudden cliff and stopped.

When she woke, she was hungry. Not again, but still. She ate some grass and a few bitter berries, and put her stomach to empty rest.

The rest of the day was desert torrid, but the late afternoon eased off into chill twilight as she lagged down the path, nearing a place she knew could be another camp. Only the canyon walls stayed warm after the sun plummeted, like another fiery shot wasted on the dark.

She had to stop to chew out a pebble between two throbbing toes of her right front paw. It came free, red and sticky as a berry. She licked the wound, too tiny to get at, or be so painful.

She struggled up again, limping both fore and aft now, like a canting seesaw. But she made it to the top of the next rock rise, where she scuffled onto a ledge and lay down, her muzzle compassed toward the cave aglow across the river.

The glow was from a campfire, and she knew that could mean friends. But there were other, stranger sparks back in the cave. These sparks winked and jigged and then gathered to cry out at the darkness. The cave pulled the cries together, and boomed them across the river, in a high-pitched tremulo that rasped her eardrums.

She shook her head in misery. She rose on her front paws, her stomach knotting with hunger, and gave full throat to her indignity.

Her angry howl bayed across the waters. They had to know she was here, had caught up with them, had gone the river, found the path, outdistanced all the danger. But the cave only gave back a terrible, trumpeting blare.

She jigged on her paws and whined at the blare, but could not keep herself down to a whine. She broke into another long howl against the screeches and scrapings and pipings and plinkings that shattered the murmurings and warbles and susurrus of the peaceful canyon.

That stopped the sounds coming from the cave.

In her brute sorrow, she bayed a third time, and the canyon dropped into riverine silence, all else subdued, except a few yapping coyotes.

She yawned to clear her ears, free them of any last

rasping out of the cave, but then heard, out of nowhere, another lilt of more insinuating shrillness.

A single note, then another, then a light trill of three notes. But this time the sound was right at hand, somewhere behind her, which made her turn her tail and growl, her blue eye sharp to starboard.

Some other piping presence hovered that near in the darkness. But she could catch no tang or odor.

The notes peeped again, prickling her ears. Beyond any range she had ever caught sounds before, like stark pings from the canyon rocks.

When the notes recurred – one, another, then that trill of three – the dog knew they were calling her.

She moved toward them, but kept her blue eye cocked, laid back her tail. They skirled higher, matching the mica glints of a moonstruck boulder that all but winked at her.

She hunched, ready to shy or spring.

A naked man rose up, speckled with the same glinting light, like mica dust, and came rocking at her. From behind the boulder, or straight out of it, she could not tell. All he wore was a big basket shoulder-strapped down the ridged knobs of his spine, and a long pipe at his lip. He kept playing as he twirled and turned, turned and twirled. The man was naked down to his thin bones, with an old, leathery skin like sun-stiffened hide stretched over them, and his white hair hung loose in long tangles, like tree moss in the moonlight. But at his groin, a large, dusky organ swung freely, keeping up the beat, right along with the other pipe.

She froze in her bristling crouch.

The man hunkered down, smiled at her like a dried-up old demon, and aimed his pipe off his lip, straight between her ears. Then his cheeks puffed once, like the strike of a adder. No sound came, but the dog rolled off her feet, whining in pain, as if actually shot at, one more time, and hit.

The man stood up, turned and twirled, and aimed the pipe again.

But the dog had already come to heel, beside his bony ankle.

Immediately the man headed upward from the boulder, angling across the rock slides with his bare, skeletal feet. The dog hestitated. She did not want to move away from the path and the river. She whined at the naked man's heels, but he turned and piped another, longer trill, straight at her.

This time his thin fingers skittered over the pipe, clutched one deep, painful note, then flipped away like twigs breaking in a rough breeze. The trill scratched a picture that she could suddenly see ahead of her. And had to pursue.

The edge of the sky
Is the home of the river

The man climbed at a fast pace, loping in long straddles from rock to rock. The perches he gained with one spindly stretch of his legs, she had to jump twice to cross, then scramble to gain. She was used to running ahead over any canyon trail, but her tongue was out in her struggle to keep up. She could still smell no scent, not even the must of age.

Soon they were high into the night sky, up among the hoodoos that the winds had carved out of the sandstone ridge. From a distance, the hoodoos looked like runaway dwarfs, stealing across the ridge, but on closer approach, they turned into miscreant giants. Wind-wizened bodies, burdened with huge heads that tipped precariously toward a great fall, yet never took one. She shadowed him, among the hoodoos, leery of being nodded at.

They arrived at a large rock window, blown open in the sandstone, also by epochal winds. Everything stood forever outside that window, which looked either way to the pale night horizon. But the old man settled himself into a corner of its rock-pillared frame. That immediately gave the window an inside. He eased the basket around his knobby shoulder, reached in for something twisted and black, and from his corner seat in the window, offered it to the panting dog.

She sniffed it once, found it noisome, then whined in an agony of hunger, sniffed again, closer, took it, and chewed. A braided string of jerky, almost too tough for her to swallow.

But the naked man stroked her throat, and it went down.

39

Carrion.

Whatever leavings the naked man could pick and shred by tracking the early circling of vultures.

She was still famished, and the noisome morsel was enough to rouse her doggedness. She turned her brown eye on him and barked, one soft gruff of needy appeal.

He smiled and tooted his pipe, soundlessly. Again a splay of three lifted fingers, broken off like twigs.

I the dog am straying

The flat rock on which she stood went wobbly, and she tilted off balance. He laughed silently as she fought for her footing against an abrupt dizziness. Another silent lilt, four fingers, flung away.

In the north wind I am straying

Then they were both up, the dog tagging after the old man, threading through the sharpening rock needles of Deso, their stone points blooded by the first reddening of dawn.

But the night would not give up its dark in the trough of the canyon, as they descended toward the sandstone ledges that hung out over a glimpse of luminous meadows, patched below them along the river.

The steep strata stood out like the dark ribs of some great lizard, burrowing underground, digging deeper with every clawing thrust.

And the river rolled off its scaled back, cooling its green skin.

On his last climb, the old man stretched to splay himself upright against the redrock, embracing a slick corner with outstretched arms, using his knobbly hands like a pair of pincers to clamp his wrinkled body to the stone. Then he eased his bony feet out along a few bare inches of cracked ridge, taking hold with only the grip of his toes.

Suddenly he was up on only one foot, all its toes. He danced, spun on their tips, hard as pebbles, until he dropped back on his rock-round heel.

Straight down were the river meadows, and at the end of the foot ridge, he swung himself out, like a gate, pivoting on that heel.

On his swing, he seized the dog by the scruff of her neck. She hung out over the canyon, all four legs kicking in midair, but caught, like some shaggy prey, in his trap-sprung fist.

He swung through a half-circle arc, still on the heel he had socketed into the ridge, and slammed himself into the far wall, like a gate thrown back on itself.

The force flung the dog into pinching blackness.

The pinch was the narrow back of a cave, where she lay trembling, until he was down again beside her. They were snuggled under a slant rock roof, and the cave opened out into the faint dawn, like a slit trench aloft, and all of the river ribboned out below them. Tailing, shimmering from far upstream, but glazed to the canyon. Flowing, yet unmoving. Slithering away, plunging on, but from where they watched, all at a stop. Even the rapids lay white and still as snow.

The old man took off his basket, squatted back on his thin hams, and laid aside his pipe. He raised a bony hand to his brow, like a gnarled fan to shade his crow-footed, jet-pointed eyes against the dawn flaring over the plateau, like a flight of fire arrows.

He lounged his free arm on what looked like an odd outcropping. But it was a wickerwork basket, canted into the cave slit, daubed in sun-dried clay. He stroked it like a woman, so shaped. Then he eased his spine up the roof wall, leaned over to loosen a thong that lifted a lid, and thrust his whole arm down inside the wickerwork.

He pulled out a handful of corn, squeezing kernels loose in his fist, like pale nuggets. He caught at them by licking his knuckles.

A few dropped down, onto her muzzle.

But only when he nodded did she lick out her own tongue to eat.

"Looked like the last I might see of her," Paul shook his head. "Or since I hadn't, all I'd ever hear of her. I tried a halloo or two, but if she'd gone back on us, what was the use of calling her in? She knew we were there. She could swim that river like a damn hippo. She'd swim it, or not, whenever she saw fit. That bothered me some after all I'd done to civilize her, but then wasn't I the one who spaced her? So I figgered float on down the river, see which one of us remembers more what really counts.

"That cave concert was done, good and over. Nobody had much heart for tootling or fiddling after her godforsaken howling. The albino tried to get something going again, but his plucking sounded real put-upon, like that harp Jack stole from the giant, keep squealing on him, all the way back down the beanstalk? Larry took a few knee swipes at her cello, but Bob up and told them both to shut it down.

"Some had a few remarks to pass about that damn dog, but I didn't sit still for them. I cornered Pam and Russ afore they snuck off to hop on top of each other and laid out a new plan. Russ and Pam to float the Chamber Pots straight down to Wriggleback, overnight there, run Flat Iron the next morning, then pull out at Nefertiti. They'd leave me off at the Ghost Ranch. And I'd give them Willie Bee, off the Knols trip, to take my place. Willie's a recovering Hari Krishna, don't fancy company too much, but he's a good boatman, and I figgered they could all three last one day together.

"Told Russ he could lead them in his kayak, 'cept for Flat Iron, where he'd have to help Pam and Willie Bee get the rafts over. He loves that yellow Dancer, works the hull with his hips, like one of them itty-bitty short skirts?"

"A tutu?" I suggested.

"Sounds right. Russ likes to slip off shore, get out in the middle river without his paddle, nothing but his own two arms. He's like the old joke about being up that creek, but keeps himself pointed by sculling with just the flat of his two hands. Won't wear his helmet. Blond hair loose to the winds, he'll stretch up both arms, lock his fingers together, overhead, then slowly roll over to the side and flip under. Puts the kayak bottom up, lets it float maybe a hundred feet downstream – we all still live in a Yellow Submarine – then does a hip roll and nips himself right straight up again.

"Damn idiot. Seen him head through Harefoot Rapid that way. Rights hisself by flipping that surfer shock of wet blond hair, at the last right moment, I swear. Lucky he don't get headlocked in a rock. Pam must think she is doing a kayak – blond hair, yellow prick – when she hunkers on him.

"But she'll keep him in order, I figger, after they leave me off at the Ghost Ranch. I got to check out the Knols kids, since I left them there to hancho around with Slocum and Willie Bee. Willie's all right, in a pinch. When he first come to me for a job, all bald, I thought he was a skinhead. A hard piece of work, but turned out he'd been doing drum and finger cymbals for the monks near a year. 'I'm off,' he told me, 'my prior religion. It done me some brain damage.' Okay by me, since he wanted to get with nature. 'Raw,' he says, 'right straight through.' I said we got plenty of that, if you don't mind lonesome, and he signed on to the river.

"Slocum I can usually dead count on, but not this time, it turns out, once I get there. We got ourselves a bad-apple kid. They don't usually turn up until you dump them all out on the ground, go over the pile to see who's got the rot spot.

"Partly again my own fault. You know about the Ghost Ranch, how the Hole-in-the-Wall Gang hid out in the ledges above there? True enough, I can quote you Wild West history on it. Butch Cassidy used to ride the boys up to the ranch, owned by a fella named Abner Carson, who never did observe nothing too close he didn't want to see. Carson had these canyon meadows and a wife named Peach, and they raised corn and hay and horses and two peach-cream daughters. One of them was supposed to be sweet on Sundance, the other on Flat Nose George, who got shot in his bedroll. Carson sat his horse crooked and was known to say, 'Out-laws are gen'rally nicer folk than the posse chasing 'em.'

"Carson had his reasons. Butch and Sundance and the others would swap horses in the dead of night, leave Carson a ten-dollar gold piece under a settled rock. Now it could of been any rock anywhere around that whole spread. Nobody can say for sure which rock, cause Carson is s'posed to keep changing the rock, ever so often, to keep the deal hid. A swindle on the law, and Carson came to no good, but it all makes a tight story.

"That's my weakness. I do like to spin a yarn around the campfire, a little scary, like Mark Twain used to tell that one about the Golden Arm? I tell these kids they can set out searching for that rock, but watch out if they find a gold piece under it. The ghost of Abner Carson will come after whoever helps hisself, at midnight. '*Who stole my gold piece?*' Then I quick grab the kid's arm next to me. '*Did you?*' He jumps a mile, they all scream, and sometimes I tell them it may be Butch or Sundance comes to you and says, '*Put it back. It ain't yourn!*'

"I leave them with that story – and Willie Bee who'll believe anything, with Slocum to keep tighter watch – but I don't realize this kid whose arm I grabbed is the one smoking weed. We get 'em sometimes, and right away we get rid of them, but this bad apple is clever sly, and we damn near lost him, it come that close.

"But I'm getting ahead of myself. I got the rest of the trip laid out, and Russ goes off with Pam for a snuggle, and I stay up more bad minutes, under the mosquito netting, thinking, why don't Blue Dog come in?

"I don't have the whole truth, or any bit of it yet, from Cat Lick on, but I already got my suspicions. Later confirmed, when I go out on a hunch and happened on to that opening in the ledges above the Ghost Ranch. I'm always on the lookout for nicks or chinks that the Old People found first around here, say, back a millennium. You can spot them from the raft if you keep your eyes peeled. Just keep scanning along the rock face till you catch a dimple, or maybe a furrow like an up-and-down frown. Anything vertical, to set it off from everything running horizontal. Mark it in your mind, and come back on a rock climb. I've found clay pots. I've found standing walls. I've found their kivas. They lived up there, just like snakes in the cracks. I can show you a spot or two when we shoot on down from here, to Nefertiti.

"But this one was a real find, on a late summer prowl, few weeks after we got that pothead kid safe back down. I wanted to see where he'd gotten hisself to, half damn stupified, beyond where they picked him up, after he come rolling into the meadows. You could call it knowing the river, or skill, but mostly pure damn luck. I was roving my eye, trying to keep the rocks inside some rough grid in my head, when I saw this swirl of swallows. They're mud-nesting, I can see that, chicks in a hive, under the ledges, but these swallows are flying straight into the cliff, plumb disappear, then somehow back out again. So I shifted 'round until I got an angle on the sun that caught this big nick, cut right out of the ledges. Looked like God sunk a wedge, one big whack.

"A slit cave, looked like you could almost stand up inside. But not quite, I found out.

"A bitch getting up there. You had to pinch your toes along this least little ridge that threads around a big slickrock bulge that takes you into the cave. I had on my old logger boots with the spikes, but the rock is rotten, just too damn risky if you ain't a swallow.

"So I took off the boots, and round that corner, you get one whopping view, up and down the whole shining river. You can see from Cat Lick and Larkspur Rapid right round to Roof Rock, then down to the meadows at the Ghost Ranch, on out to Wriggleback, with that spew of boulders out of the draw that flumes down here to Flat Iron, and from there almost to Nefertiti.

"And right straight across, at eye level, is dead solid flatland. Nothing but the plateau. However much you feel like you been climbing mountains, you get to see how far down a big crack you been.

"The Old People had this cave for their balcony seat. They hunkered, took in a few rays and glommed the river view. Tell you what else they had going. That slant rock roof has been pecked over, every damn inch, like a graffiti mural. It is crawling with two-fanged rattlers and flying eagles and flat-footed lizards and curly-tailed scorpions and geometrics and squawfish and bear

49

paws and so many antlers and arrows, you couldn't move in there without getting bit or stung or clawed or zinged somehow. Real rock art.

"Best of all, dead center of the roof, is this big reptile. Like a giant turtle with four big web feet and a long, pointy tail and his nasty-nosed head stuck forward. But it ain't boxed like a turtle. It's stretched out, what do you call it? Eee-long-gated. And running zigzag down its back, you can see its squiggly ridgebone taking all the meanders you can see right down below.

"That ridgebone is the river, I swear. Rising sun hits it dead the same way, only earlier, over the plateau. Could be a damn map.

"I figger this balcony is also their pew. The Old People got their magic up here, crawling on the roof, prolly got some shaman to come visit, get a fix on the river, so it treats them right. Good thinking, I say.

"And what else do I find, still intact, like the day before we got here they wove it out of river rushes? One of their granaries. Woven and mudded up, with a lift lid. Come to pray, stay to eat. I even find corn. Hard as nailheads, but if you can crack it, you can eat it. We're talking like the pharoah's wheat in those pyramids. That corn is alive, you can still grow an Indian stalk with them. Done that in my own garden.

"But what strikes me, I don't just find corn in the granary, but outside, scattered on the ledge. Only a few kernels, but that's what the swallows come after, right?

"Only how come it's scattered? Who's been into the

50

granary? Lid's tight down, must be recent, or the swallows would of had it all by now.

"Then what do I see, back under the rock roof, nearly out of sight. Even though it's a few weeks old, a familiar shape.

"Dog luck."

Paul stood up, dusting his palms, you could see excited. He does love to tell you the best part of a story. "Now how is a dog gonna get in there? No four-foot has a chance on that thread ridge. Somebody carried that dog. And 'less she jumped halfway across Deso into the damn river, somebody also hauled her out of there. Somehow. Want you to see something, down here, other side of that rock."

He got me up, politely dragging me along for company, talking his way around to the far side of this squared-off white limestone.

Much as I expected, it was decorated blue-white space. Some pictographs, distinct stick figures, scored on the limestone in white and red. Primitive art, I'm told, but it always looks to me like play school. Like some kid drew them with hot tar on the end of a twig.

"Look at this fella," Paul points to the largest stick figure. Bulbous, with the round basket on its back, and holding a cross-stroke between two other curved upstrokes. That's primitive art for this stick guy is holding something in his two hands, with one end up to his round head, which is primitive art for the same stick guy is playing the flute.

"And here's the spout," Paul points to another down-stroke, this one off its round belly, long and tapered. "To the gene pool."

That's primitive art for a formidable penis. I had to admit it was one of the better Kokopelli I'd seen drawn, following raw nature.

"Now I know all you're gonna say, and you can say it," Paul began making excuses. "But I could swear something like that's what's got to of happened to her," he kept tapping below the sketch, knowing what a wild claim he was staking.

"She ran into one of the Old People."

It was the dog who woke to sounds of howling.

Human howling. Close and forlorn, weeping out loud. Then a catch of hysterical gulps, and silence again.

She yawned a low whine and licked her lips, back on starboard watch. The naked man had already risen. He was crawling out on his hands and knees, to hang his head far over the cave drop, to listen hard.

Another tearful howl, cut short by a begging sob.

The old man hopped up on his stone heels. He crinkled his eyes to stare at the climbing sun, now angling steep morning into the canyon. He held his right arm straight up, like a gnomon, and studied its arrowpoint shadow on the brightening rock roof. The point quivered in a bend of the wriggling curve that ran down the back of the turtle.

When he was satisfied with their alignment, he took up his pipe and puffed once at the dog. She came to him instantly.

He reached into his basket and pulled out another string that smelled like jerky. But when the dog bit for it, he grabbed her front legs and flipped her neatly over on her back. She kicked at him, but he was already winding the greasy string of braided hemp around her forepaws. She whined and struggled, but feebly, and he looped her back legs with the hemp, and trussed all four paws together, like the mouth of a black sack.

He squatted lower, piping to her again until she was calm. Then he bowed his moss-strewn head and pushed it through her bound legs. He lifted off his hams, all the while patting her head, cradling her against his chest.

Very slowly, he eased her head over his right shoulder until her limp body slung around onto his back, the knot of her paws against his throat. He tested her hang, just as he would have hitched at the basket he usually carried on his shoulders. Satisfied again, he stooped out of the cave and toed onto the narrow ridge. He worked his feet by inches, hunching his shoulders against the drag of her body, hooking at studs and cracks with talonous fingers.

Once around the slickrock facing, he did not release her. He kept her slung on his back and started a perilous descent away from the sun, down the slickrock. More sure-footed on two legs than she on four.

The howling still reached them, from time to time, but it was diminishing into despair. He hurried toward its seeming source, tracing an aural pathway with a keen ear for deceiving echoes. It led him nearer the dark buildings that sat in the yellow meadow below, their swollen boards sprung from passing storms, or other visits of violence.

Men had once come to live along the river, claiming the very flow of its waters, but now they only came to build brief fires between floating down, floating away.

He could see some of them gathered around a curl of smoke. Others were running in among the rocks, but not far enough to reach the howling. They were like large ants that could not climb, only scurry.

He dropped down nearer the howling, then caught a frightened whimpering, somewhere off to his right. He moved up again, toward a break of pinyon and juniper, keeping low, bracing with his knees, until he could see down through the blue-green branches what their overhang hid.

There was a ledge under the jut of the junipers, and a red-haired boy turning rigid, then trembling, then rigid again.

He could also see where a piece of the ledge had slipped away, like a soft wedge of crumbs, near the boy's foot.

The boy could neither turn around nor go forward. He had his big sneaker heels dug back into the ledge, and both his arms were stretched out against the cliff wall. Mostly all dark sweater, the sleeves torn and sprung and sagging. And weeping steadily, a rain of childish tears, but could not let go of the cliff wall to wipe his eyes.

The boy was bodily petrified, but also gave spastic signs of dizziness. He did not seem to know where he was, nor how to stop the unknown place from starting to spin around and around with him.

The old man slipped the dog from his shoulder, but did not untie her. He put his pipe to his lip, aiming it like a bobbing branch through the junipers, in a lower key both the boy and the dog could hear. His fingers flicked, tossing away the tune.

I swing the spirit like a child

She tried to shake the irritating sound out of her ears, but the boy responded to the notes like balm flowing down over the hardrock world around him. His sobbing eased. He could draw breath again, over his gulps of hysteria.

But the notes also made the boy curiously sleepy. He looked dreamy and alert, both at the same time. His arms began to lose their rigidity, freeing his hands to finger-creep back along the rough cliff face. But he still could not move his feet.

The man reached down and yanked once, untying the dog's legs. She untangled herself, spraddled up, and he puffed the pipe sharply at her twice between the ears. The boy could not hear, but she did, and gave a bark.

The boy heard that.

"Up here, up here!" he cried out.

The man gave her a shove in the hinders with his hard-heeled foot and sent her downward with flicking fingers. Then he turned and skirled his pipe to tamp down the boy's panic again.

The dog half tumbled out of the junipers, broke her

descent by agile footwork on a hummock of lichen at the far end of the ledge. She turned her brown eye toward the boy, who stared back at her in tearful disbelief.

"Here doggy, good doggy, here here here!"

But she lay down, right where she was, edging both front paws onto the crumbly ledge.

The piping kept up, rendering the boy both dazed and determined. He did not really know where he was going, but his feet started to move, bellying along the ledge, like a pair of rock animals. One sneakered foot scuffed toward the dog who had barked, driven by these strange sounds that were somehow encouraging him. Then the other sneakered foot dragged after the first, and that one started to scuff forward again.

When another soft wedge of crumbs dropped away, right between his two large sneakers.

His arms sprang wide to the cliff wall again. He was banging his red hair against it, trying to beat back through the rock.

The pipe struck off more unheard notes, among leaf breezes from the junipers, and the dog instantly got up.

She barked at the boy again. Then slowly walked out onto the crumble and lowered her muzzle, as if waiting to be petted.

"Good doggy, good doggy, good doggy!" the boy wept.

He took one trembling hand off the rock and reached down for the ruff of her neck. He could not help himself. He grabbed hold of her, for dear life, in a furry fistful.

She set all four legs, quite as if expecting this all along. She raised her muzzle, letting him still keep his clutch hold on her ruff, and gently took her own hold on his sweater cuff with her long canines.

Then she pulled firmly. He scuffed forward, whimpering. She pulled again, and he scuffed again. Slowly, first pull, then scuff, she backed up, bringing him, a footfall at a time, along the crumbling ledge.

Until he fell forward in a panicky stumble, over the hummock, and she straddled him to make sure he was safe.

She waited for the hidden man to come out of the break, but he did not appear. She barked, on her own, at the junipers. There was no signal back, not a stir in the greenery, and no peep from the pipe, heard or unheard.

Instead, the boy began to roll away. Deliberately, out from under her legs. Still half giddy, he was turning over and over toward the leveling ground, shrieking with delight.

He gained a slow speed downhill, his red hair flaming like the untrimmed wick of a candle, and others were running uphill.

She saw them coming, and barked a sharp warning, to keep them off. But the boy was already up on his knees, his arms raised high and shrieking at them with half-crazed laughter.

She knew them, and hesitated. They might still be friends. They could wrestle head to head, and chase down the sandy shoreline together, and trust themselves to willful play with a broken stick tossed to the river. *Go get it, Blue!* But she had caught something hostile in the acrid, low-curling smoke from their camp-fire, saw in their fast approach a guise, a hurried cloak over capture.

She was not afraid. She stood her ground, let them reach the boy. But when he pointed wildly at her, and they looked altogether up her way, she let loose an abrupt, canny howl. Then turned and loped back into the junipers, out of their sight or any reach.

"This kid's name is Matthew, a New York City spoiled rich snotass. We get them all the time. The school catches them smoking dope, so whichever parent's got custody, or at least knows where the kid hangs out, sends us the snotass for the Great Out-of-Doors to straighten out. Sometimes it works. We sure as hell try. But some of them bring their stash, and if you don't shake them down, they get high – somewhere high up, worse than perilous – and do themselves harm. And then their shit-tailed parents goddamn sue.

"Anyhow, this Matt is sly. With big brown freckles, a redhead charm ball. When I give the lecture at the start of the trip, blister them good on no substances, he comes up, all humble. He's got this waterproof tobacco pouch, full of weed, asks me, 'Will you keep this for me till after the trip?' I take it from him, unfold it, dump the stuff out right there. 'You know you're breaking the law,' I tell him. 'Don't ask me to.' He gives me a look. I give him back the empty pouch, Dunhill, expensive, then he nods, still more humble. 'Okay, okay,' he all but beams, and I fell for it.

"I tell Willie Bee, right in front of him, Matt's come clean. End of that first day, at the Ghost Ranch, I sit him down at campfire, next to me. I forgot what these schools really teach their New York smartasses. Whatever else they may flunk, these kids ace Greed and Lying. They get their degree in it. And here I am telling him whoppers about where to find that ten-dollar gold piece. Our boy Matt figgers this trip ain't gonna be wasted, he'll go for the gold, all on his own. After he gets high on the other half of his stash, which of course he's held back.

"Why should Willie Bee or Slocum keep watch on Matt, once I'd spoken for him? But if I'm falling for Matt's story, Matt is buying into mine. He has it down pat that everybody else been looking in the wrong place. That gold piece won't be found on the ranch because no stone's been left unturned. Not around the outbuildings, nor out in the meadow. That's Matt's way of thinking, and he's been to a good school. He's gonna take off after that trail Butch and Sundance wormed up to their Hole in the Wall, which hole I for one ain't never found.

"A long way up that trail's got to be where the stone is, Matt figgers. Butch likely left that gold piece where it'd cause Abner Carson some stint to collect. Matt even asks Willie Bee where that trail is. Willie Bee gives him bullfeathers about a draw up canyon toward the top of the plateau, too tough for novices, so Matt is buying into more stories.

"We get all these embellishments after we got him

safe back down. Not us, really. Blue Dog done it, if you can half believe Matt, and I do, this once. As for who else saved his sorry little candy ass, God knows if you can credit the rest of what he spits out.

"By the time I float there from Roof Rock with the Chamber Pots, Matt is already back down, but still raving. I ask Willie Bee, how'd this happen? 'Cliffed hisself,' Willie Bee snaps at me, 'and your dog rolled him down to us.' I sit down with Matt, and I can see he is still high. I shake my head at Willie Bee but more at myself. Matt is awed still to be alive, but scared to say what he really seen, mostly heard up there on that cliff.

"What's clear is he vamoosed after camp breakfast, which he didn't eat but smoked his own, striking for the trail where Willie Dee pointed him. 'It kept on winding up,' he says to us, 'winding along, and I always thought it was gonna stretch out flat over the next rise, but it didn't. I kicked over stones that looked likely, and I seen, like, glints.' You bet he did, him and his dope. 'But I can't find the right one until I'm going way up and out and around on this gleam from all the glints that turns into a tiny little crumbling path I can't move my feet on.'

"Don't even know he's gone out on a ledge. Cliffs hisself, up seven hundred feet on that rotten-rock face above the ranch. A lot of height, and a sheer drop, no way back or forwards. The dope keeps telling him to drop off the cliff into sweet dreams, so he starts screaming his lungs out.

"That's what they hear down below, but he is hearing something else. Already spinning around with his feet froze, he hears this twittering. 'It's like some bird, but it's singing too good to be a real bird, not like one that flies.' I'm starting to get the picture. Too many notes to be a jay or a cowbird or some canyon thrush. But enough to be a funny picture I'm getting, half a ghost of an idea – which is what you're seeing right there on this ceremonial rock."

Paul is pointing to the Kokopelli, waggling his finger at the cross-stroke that stands for music in primitive art.

"Matt don't see him if he's there. All he hears is birdsong out of the bushes, that somehow makes him feel better. 'It's like a lullaby bird?' he says, or the dope says it for him. What's real is the dog comes for him. 'Oh man, was I glad to see that doggy,' he blubbers. 'Big as a horse. Do I love that doggy.'

"He is up there clinging to the cliff that is like a piece of dried-out cheese, so that's how Blue Dog looks to him. Digs his hands into Blue Dog's fur for dear life, starts crying again. 'Doggy grabs my sleeve,' he shows us the tear, then he has this sudden change of heart. 'Goddamn dog didn't have to rip my sweater!' That's how high he's doped. 'Look what your goddamn dog done to my cuff!'

"Matt's gone hopeless weepful, and is dozing off on the dope, so Willie Bee tells me the rest. 'We been searching half the morning, trying to fix on his crying

64

jag, but Blue Dog brought him in.' Then Willie Bee give me a look as bald as he is, with no smile. 'We tried to call Blue Dog, hitch hold of her, but she was gone.'

" 'Can't be helped,' I tell him.

" 'What's with her?'

" 'Picked up a new master.' Willie Bee is giving me less than no smile. 'If I were to guess, it could be one of the Old People.'

"That don't make any kind of sense to Willie Bee, but it does to Slocum, who I also got with the Knols kids. I shunt Willie Bee off to the Chamber Pots, and keep Slocum on hand. He come to these parts from Wyoming where he drove scrub cattle and hardheads out of the Wind Rush for loose change at the BLM roundup. He is a cowpoke turned river guide, still likes to herd people, takes hard after any strays who try to cut out on him. Slocum can see Matt is a problem, but can also see I got a bigger problem with my dog that's only gonna get settled some downriver way by Deso, not by him or me or Willie Bee. He tucks back his big Stetson – gallons of hat in the crown, no bigger sombrero on the river – so far back it makes him look like he's got this wide-brim halo.

" 'What you wanna do with this doper?'

"That I already got solved. I am waiting on Jeff Harrington with that Piper one-lung, while I get Russ and Pam and Willie moving off downriver with the Chamber Pots, all three rafts, headed to overnight at Wriggleback. 'You can take point in the kayak,' but again I tell Russ, 'Back off, and help Pam and Willie run them through, when you get to Flat Iron.'

"Best I get them out of here, seeing Slocum pull down his hat at the very sight of Russ, let alone Pam. So far down, that Stetson's blocking out all his eyesight. 'Don't care for Yalies,' Slocum holds, 'any more than fillies.' It's a mystery what you get on the river. Slocum never out of his jeans, but those two can't keep from jumping into each other's.

"About that time, we get the rafts launched, and Russ is paddling away, working like the wings on a water bug. Then we hear the buzz. From up canyon comes the hopper, hugging the wind, lining on the meadow to land against the way the grass is blowing. Quite a sight, that Piper one-lung coming in low over the flotilla of rafts, on a slowpoke downriver. Piper looks so thin landing, like a weesome bird coming straight at you, but it touches down big as any farm machine, and the prop wash puddles through the yellow meadow, like stirring up a dry pot of gold.

"I call a meeting, over by the Ghost Ranch forge, a rust pile of hack-toothed saws and no-good implements and a plowshare that must've once or twice turned over the meadow. Who'd want to godforsaken farm out here? You have to think Abner Carson is better off a ghost, be glad both his daughters upped and run off. That reminded me of what I had to lay down for these other kids, gathered round.

"'Matt is off this trip,' I tell them. 'You know the

66

rules, now you see why we have rules. Matt cost you a whole morning of downtime, and if it hadn't been for Blue Dog, Matt'd still be up there, or maybe fallen down those rocks.' And I shuddered to think of it.

" 'Where's your dog?' one of them asks.

" 'Still seeing that no more of you get into a pile of trouble. And see that you don't. No more hunting gold pieces, they ain't nothing but tall tales anyhow. Sorry I told you them.'

"They were stirring something sullen, but I could see I was making my point, sharp enough. 'You want to go off somewhere, you follow behind Slocum. He's your guide, nobody else. Each and every one of you keeps in line, from now on, or we haul the lot of you off like Matt.' Then I had to add. 'And if you see my dog, call her in and hang onto her, better than Matt did.'

" 'Matt says she bites,' I hear.

" 'She saved Matt's life, who wouldn't know if a snake bit him, he's so stoned. Do I make myself heard?'

"There was silence, which is at least better than aggravation. I turned them back over to Slocum, who gives them a lot of hat. Then I took aholt of Matt by his torn sweater sleeve, and elbow-marched him to the plane, at a hot, hard trot to make him look more like a prisoner than some hero. He stumbled right along, and I shoved him into the rear seat, ready to stuff myself next to Jeff Harrington in the cockpit.

"Got to admit, it's a thrill every time, lifting out of that canyon meadow. I draw down hard on the prop, and Jeff kicks her into idle, then rudders her tail around in a swirl of golden straw. I get in, and we roll off. It's like running a comb through that whole stretch of meadow. Then he turns and makes a cowlick, revs her hard, and heads her into the wind.

"We are plowing through golden grass almost up to the wing struts, and that engine is chugging windsprints. But we lift off light as a seed on its whirly wings, I swear, rock walls on either wingtip. Jeff banks up and away when we go hard against the headwall, takes her back over the Ghost Ranch.

"I look down, and they are waving. I look over my shoulder, quick at Matt, and he is waving back. Coming out of the dope, smiling hooray, and I can see what's passing between him and his buddies back down on the ground. They're all wondering, 'How come you get the plane ride, after being so badass?'"

The dog could not find the naked man with her nose.

Dry bones, still drier skin left no scent back in the junipers, and nothing haunted the wind behind his swift escape down the canyon.

She could only track him, intermittently, by those distant trills like birdsong. They pealed at her, then damped away into canyon echoes, then rose higher to excruciating taunts – beyond human hearing, but not her own. They drew her on, these eerie pipings that loosed tiny dirt spills down the pitched walls, out of wee cracks and shifts and pops in the striated rock.

Through the hammering heat, she hunted after him with her head raised, ears painfully perked, seldom lowering her muzzle.

He was headed into the deepest cut at a breakneck pace, enticing her with his ephemeral chirrups. Down the long blaze of remaining day, he kept moving from the great uplifts of paged slate, onto the white sandstone that curled over the red rock like ages of icing on a darkly layered cake. Interminable rains had sluiced torrents over these sandstone margins, off into the river, leaving black stains of desert varnish like ghostly downspouts.

Near dusk, she crossed the last white table, again badly limping, her sides heaving and her tongue lolling.

From afar, the rimrock backed deep into a high-walled corner, also blackened with desert varnish. But on nearer approach, these walls became whitely peopled. Tall, shag-limbed figures loomed in ropy ranks, like tattered but menacing specters. Long ago, they had been pecked out of the black varnish, dinted down to the white sandstone by the flaking and chipping of many hands. Then a colorless rainbow had been scored in a rude arch over these rock-born spirits. The many scorings entrapped them there, caught in the web of some godlike spider.

It was sacred ground, guarded by round white eyes and brute shoulders hanging swales of legs without feet. One of the specters soared a ghoulish head taller than the others, fronting a mad, trapezoidal stare. A white beast jumped at its side, with paws and a stump tail and raised ears and a lifted muzzle.

She halted, turning her blue eye on these vagaries of resemblance. Then the specter took up a mad sway, and she growled at its threats from the wall, and the naked man stepped forward.

He came once more out of the rock, a basket slung again from his shoulders, and seated himself cross-legged on a white sandstone pillow. He had been somewhere and back. His hand gestured her to come to him as he piped a soft warble at her, like a canyon swallow.

Blue Dog, Green River

The crest of the mountain
Forever remains
Forever remains
Though the rocks continually fall

He nodded his head, like a tilting rock, and she rose and crawled into his lap.

There she settled between the angled bones of his spread legs, into the burrow they made, shaded from the last sinking burst of sunlight by his hunched shoulders, under the arch of the rock rainbow.

Out of exhausted impulse, she licked his knee. Her tongue rasped against wrinkled skin, like rough bark, but she kept licking. He reached into her matted fur. His hand was like a rake, clawing through the tangles, but the harrowing brought a welcome ease.

Then his hand came away from her fur and began fingering in the cracks of the sandstone. He picked something loose, small but alive and kicking, and held it near her nose, deftly, between his skeletal fingertips. She recoiled.

A sand-colored scorpion, whipping its tail, like a fiery barb.

She tried to scramble free, but his knees clamped shut. He held her in their vise, raised the scorpion away from her nose and, again deftly, pinched it dead. He pulled off the two tiny claws with his teeth, spitting them out. Then he began twirling the scorpion between bony fingertips, crimping its stinger to a finer

point. At the same time, he ringed her muzzle with his free hand, clamping down on her snout with his thumb. Once she stopped quivering, he jabbed the dead scorpion's broached stinger into her left hinder.

She shook with the hot pain, but could not kick or whine against it. She could only twitch. He used both knees and now both hands to restrain her convulsing body, until the growl caught back in her throat, like grinding gravel, then stopped altogether.

She was numb, but dropping strangely out of pain. When he eased his grip on her muzzle, her tongue flicked gingerly out between her teeth. He let go, let her lick his knee again.

Then he crooked his elbow, over his shoulder into his basket, and pulled out another braid of jerky. She bit into its smoky weave, and he stroked her throat again, but this time she nearly gagged on its pungency. The bitter slake of dried blood.

Man corn.

What had made this ground sacred was butchery. These were the slaughtering rocks, where he had always brought his enemies, other Anasazi. He fed her, as he did himself, on dried pullings from their stripped flesh. It was medicine. After the sting of the needle.

As her pain lessened, along with her hunger, so did her fatigue. She felt her body stretching out into a long sling, hung from her spine, between the two hard knobs of his knees. One knee which she kept licking, the other where her tail beat roughly.

Then she felt the sling slowly rocking. It rocked the sting out of her left hinder and the hurt out of her paws, the ache out of her heaving chest.

She bucked her head to round her brown eye upward, on the face of the old man.

His white hair was hanging over her, and the whites of his eyes bore down on her like the staring walls, but unlike the walls, he was smiling. He was brought alive by his gleaming teeth and startling eyes under luminous locks, like gathered fox fire.

She felt his white warmth through the canyon chill. The chill and the warmth came together with the bitterroot of man corn and the sting of the scorpion thorn. She lay there, slowly rocking, slowly healing.

Around them, the canyon itself rocked into darkness, under the sway of the swiftly passing sky. They were down at the bottom of a gigantic rift cut in the earth's crust by eroding winds and water, and over them, the night drove the stars in their constellations like cattle across a draw.

They looked up into twinkling hoofbeats.

While below them, the river dug its claws still deeper into bedrock, its green back glistening.

They rocked together, beyond all brute barriers. The river scourged the canyon, scraping sand and silt over the mured floor, carving a deeper cleft out of the immobile stone, scoring endless channels for its ceaseless pulse. That pulse beat everywhere, touched everything, sent the river through the rock to run through the spine of the sleeping dog, into the bent back of the old man, who raised his pipe to his lip to stream those ripples back again into the lowering night.

I the song I am walking here

Strange names are queathed this endless flow of runnels and rivulets. They are deemed to be systems – *solar* or *continental* or *drainage* or *limbic* – but it is always the same river. It is always the Green.

Even when the earth quakes and lifts its back upon trembling mountains, that river rises again. To scour the canyon, bore through clay and rock and flesh and bone, and braid the endless trickles that drive all living things to look up, out of their deepening cracks in the earth, for some brief glimpse of the escaping stars.

The dog was long asleep when the naked man sprang up, tumbling her onto the rimrock.

A terrible bluish light arced, spit blindingly, then turned everything into pelting rain, before they heard the split-rock crack of thunder.

The dog's fur stood up in fire points. The old man bellowed at the storm, even as its winds tore at his white scalp, hurled rain to tap into his skull.

Already water was sheeting across the sandstone. She struggled to keep her footing, while the flood lapped the man's twig ankles, climbing his shins. But he kept staring into the furioso of the cloudburst, turning round and round, awash in a circle, to find its roaring heart.

75

Then he thrust his thin arm at a dark spot, like a black bruise in the roiling clouds. Out of it whipped another stroke of lightning, stropping more thunder, but already moving off from them.

The old man turned to run after the cloudburst, splashing a track of bare-heeled puddles. The dog skittered behind him.

The storm kept to its scourging path, striking off to grasp at a near pinnacle, forming a fist of clinging fog.

Behind them, the flood folded over itself in rippling windrows, sluiced toward the rimrock, and rushed away down the spout stains. Rain streamed across the wall, giving a sudden shimmer of movement to these white spirits, but their wavy scintilla soon flattened back into the dry inertia of aging rock.

Then came a last flurry of drizzle, then nothing at all. The remaining slick, roused by the first heat of the rising sun, soon steamed into mist, turning the world back into desert again.

"You get a good view from that Piper one-lung. Side-panel windows are too small, but when Jeff leans the Piper over on them, it's all laid out for you. You got no idea what down here looks like from way up there." Paul kept on, stuck with his story, no matter where it was taking him. "You can really see the river's green. Live green, like the green is floating, actually growing in it. Takes a lot of meanders through Deso afore it runs into Grey Canyon. Like a green snake. Where it reaches the Colorado, down at the confluence, over that broad beach full of river stones, all rounded off like flat cannon balls, that you got to hike acrost to see the two rivers join up?

"That's where I say the Colorado gets snake bit by the Green, and acts crazy wild, from there on out. Carries the poison live on down to L. A.

"What I'm watching on that flight back to Moab, late that day, is how my parties are stretched out along the Green. Slocum has the Knols kids doing cleanup at the Ghost Ranch, minus this bad apple we got bucketed back of me. Good for nothing 'cept to press for cider.

"Then on down a few riffles, nothing too ferocious, I can see Russ's yellow Dancer leading the three rafts of Chamber Pots. They look still, not moving, same as the rapids, which always look like white lace. Russ is gonna put in at Wriggleback, which is that side canyon we just passed, back a ways, short of Flat Iron here.

"That Wriggleback is one narrow-hipped canyon. The overhang is so bad some places that its walls lean over, slide right into each other. You got vines and juniper and box elder and willow, some tamarisk growing so thick acrost, it cuts off the sun like somebody don't want the light of day ever falling down there. It's a real shadowy dark squeeze but when it floods, Wriggleback can pitch out boulders like a slot paying off a fruit row. That's how you get rapids, and that's why you see Flat Iron running so much white water."

Paul raised a hand to the sizzle. He likes to talk hydrology.

"At its fiercest, it's a number-five rapid, no question about it. That's how it's always been. Every year Wriggleback throws out a handful of rocks, and the river plays havoc and the odds with them.

"Come high water, early spring, that current is a real powerhouse. You got to know how a river works. It picks up on itself, runs faster up top than down at the bottom. That river is layered, same as the rocks are, only every layer is moving. Every foot-and-a-half layer of water takes speed from all the other layers under it. Then adds its own speed. It's like a mountain moving

down a channel. The deeper the water, the faster you're skimming along up top.

"That's why when you dig your oar deep down, it takes hold. You got the blade into slower water. You can lock on it, gives you the leverage to control your raft. Raft is always on the go, trying to give you the slip. But dig the blade down there into deeper water, you can turn her right the way around, like a daisy in a whirl.

"I'm watching Pam do that, direct below us, turning the raft over to Wriggleback. Back up the river, I can see another party pulling out at Catlick. From Marv's big shiner barge. They ain't made much progress. We swoop low, and even from up in the plane, they don't look right. They're weaving and running around, getting nothing accomplished, and I wave to Thai Chee, who is trying to chase them like goats. I don't know any part of it yet, but that gets me to worrying about Blue Dog again.

"Can I maybe spot her from up here? Ideal, you'd think, but how do you find a black spot anywhere in all that Deso rock pile – all those terraces and tables and half-moon slivers of beach – when nothing looks like it's moving, even the river?

"That's the one trouble. From up there, everything you see is like a petroglyph. It's dead still, same as rock art. All you're really doing is a fancy lot of glyphing.

"And what am I looking for? Some wild beast, gone back on me? Is she on a blood hunt? Or is she moving in that other world I swear I know is down there?

Though I never seen one myself, maybe heard his flute, 'cept on the sides of rocks. Like I can see them right down there, leaning up against that varnish wall, off Scorpion Pinnacle, like a ghost squad.

"I tell Jeff let's buzz once more upriver, and he lets down low, and we scared up a couple great blue heron. Look like them damn big bat dinosaur birds – what you call them?"

"Pterodactyls," I said.

"That's them, come to haunt Deso. We even scared up a bighorn ram off one of the benches, jumping high with his two big curled horns, like – those baskets you always see spilling fruit and stuff out on the table-cloth?"

"Cornucopias," I said.

"What the hell's that ram doing down here with the pedestrians? Then once we got so low to the river I could see a bunch of carp piling on top of each other.

"But no Blue Dog.

"That's about all else I can see when we zoom up, bank back toward Moab, so Jeff can land on the mesa. It's a big bake of crumble cake, all it's got is one red candle that's the air sock. All I can see is shot-through blue weather, 'cept this one little dark patch rigged up behind Wriggleback.

"'Looks like a squall,' says Jeff, who don't ever say one word he don't have to.

The dog and the old man were running together, trying to catch the rain.

They gave chase all across the white sandstone crust, until the storm swerved cagily to dodge them. It took a vagrant turn, backing off from the river, driving beyond the pinnacle.

Up ahead, they saw its dark, pelting curtain draw together, then disappear thunderously, dragging its last windy skirts of rain around the pinnacle.

So it became a hunt.

They could still hear distant crackling and the beat of rain. And the dog could smell its humid, heaving odor, soon enough picked up the wet tracks of the thunderhead.

She forged ahead of the old man, with a sudden, dizzying energy, and nosed her muzzle down, stretching her stride to run, jump, stop, swerve, run, stop, run, and jump.

They hunted around the drag-faulted pinnacle that anchored the east wall of the canyon, where the meandering river writhed almost back upon itself. She led him up these shaled turnings, around their ziggurat, still strewn with mists from the running storm. She stopped at the topmost twist and sniffed the wind for fresher signs of moisture.

She caught the mixed, hot tang of ozone and cloud, somewhere off to the north. That disoriented her, since they were striking south, until she dropped further around the backside of the pinnacle into a laggard mist. There was its spoor. The rain had crept down from the pinnacle, then back from the river cliffs on its sly retreat away from them.

It was skulking, seeking a hideout.

She cast her starboard blue eye, then ran full out, trusting the old man to keep pace. She felt cured, like a resuscitant, once again at her own loping strength. Her paws dug into the pointed shales, but she did not feel their cut. Her heart thrummed in her chest, and her black tail flagged out like a lancer's colors.

She ran hard through a mist patch that turned again to pelting rain, then caught the storm at the rim of the side canyon. Lightning slashed and ripped down through the canyon's tangled overhang, and rain poured into the dry gulch. Thunder walloped off its shrieking walls.

Then, before their very eyes, the turbulence sank slowly into the canyon, sucked low by a down draft.

From the rock rim, they could watch the storm struggle for life, boiling in its own cauldron. Lightning did it self-injury, until its violence was choked off, drowned in lashings of torrential rain. A rain that did not fall. It erupted, snatching at box elder and willow and tangling vine. Viciously tearing everything to wrack, then scratching hard again to gorge on whatever else could be gouged loose, turned to mud.

They heard slathering down rock walls and a rising gush as the canyon began to run, then the rumble of water moving toward flood. They saw the storm's last force churn this moil into a foam-lipped wave. Saw that wave pick up deadfall and boulders, clicking them together like sticks and stones.

The old man thrust his angry arms over the rim, shaking both fists at the torrent below. He rose and trotted one way, the other way in his fury, but could find no approach, no bridge over the whipping overhang.

He kept rocking in bob with the wave's tumbling plunge down the canyon. The dog cocked her blue eye at him and saw that he stood stymied like a hoodoo, teetering too near the edge, but too far away to cross.

She saw the naked man had an old rock's fear of waters at flood.

All of a tremble, he turned back from the draw and knelt to the dog, who gave him more blue eye. Down on his knees, he raised his pipe to play a flight of woodnotes.

She whined and pawed at him.

The woodnotes keened upward, hit silence, but he went on cruelly piping.

She bounded to her feet, kept on bounding away

from the painful keening, but shied at yet another silent lilt, fell desperately to pawing at her ears to shake off its dire demand.

The sky will fall
The red water eddies

But she could not. She bounded back, and cut her hard run into a circle around the piping man, pushing with all her muscle against the hold of his ululation.

The pipe sang a quick picture.

The little red ant
comes down the mountain
with only one arrow

He spun at dead center of a tightening circle, twirling his neck and head after her racing blackness. Still piping at her, driving her nearer the rim. Kept her barreling around at full heft, into a heaving shoulder tilt, until she was headed on a galloping tangent, straight for the overhang.

He puffed both cheeks once.

A single note, like a blown dart.

She leapt.

"See that rooster tail, river left?"

Paul was up on the Navajo sandstone outcropping, like a lectern. Taking a pause in his story, to line us up for our own run at Flat Iron. Or so I thought.

"See how it keeps changing shape, but stays always in one place? That's the difference between any river and the ocean. An ocean wave moves, but a river wave stays. Always in the same place, but never the same twice. You hear tell about this chaos theory – those newfangled fractions they got now?"

"Fractals," I said.

"That's them, but it ain't them. I got my own theory. It starts with that first drop that melts off the snowcap back at the riverhead, way up there in Wyoming, until that drop reaches here and tucks up in that rooster tail. May look like some cockadoodle feather" – he tossed a rock straight into the frothing spout – "but it's the pulse of the river."

Paul picked up another rock. "That drop of water never had but one choice to make. Back up in Wyoming, right the moment it melted loose from the snowpack, does it head southeast for the Mississippi, or veer off northwest to the Columbia, or does it take its chances on trickling our way down the Green? And since that drop already made up its mind long ago, here it is, flipping up in that rooster tail afore it pops off to the Colorado.

"Now, see that V running river right of that rooster tail? Once you're into that V, you got to paddle hard river left, just shave past the rooster tail, cause that lateral is gonna drive you river right into" – he heaved, on a high trajectory, and the splash disappeared into a white yawning in the rapid – "that godforsaken hole."

Paul pointed me down its gulping mouth. "Know what causes holes? Vacuums. Water running so fast over big rocks that it gets sucked backwards. And backwards against the main current reverses the wave and ends up taking you straight down. Holes can grab you hard." He picked up another rock. "They're either smiles or frowns. If you get caught in a smile, okay. Sooner or later, it will let you out, one corner of its smile or the other. But if you're caught in a frown, that's another matter. Take you everything you've got to paddle your way out of a frown. As you can readily see, that hole" – he pegged again into the thrashing yawn – "is a damn frown."

We both gave it our regard, how we'd best slip by, once back in our kayaks. But Paul still had his story in mind, kind of like water on the brain.

"Wicked enough frown, on any ordinary run, like we're taking. But you get a flash flood come pouring out of Wriggleback, it swoles up the whole river, right sudden, then the rapids. You got a frown deep enough to drown all the sorrows you ever knowed. And next to it, don't look for that rooster tail. You got a pumphouse geyser.

"That squall set it off, the one Jeff spotted from up over the mesa. Funny thing about those summer squalls. They're like hermits. Shaggy and dirty and sneaky and lonesome. Out for theirselves. You'll see them creeping across the canyonlands, threatening to come down here and there, but mostly their rain don't never reach the ground. All you see is the thunderheads turning grey bellied. They just sort of perspire. Along the rocks, the most you ever see is their sweat trail.

"But Jeff spots this squall already dropping down. What this squall's doing is looking for somewhere to hole up. Same way a hermit scoots into a cave. A squall like that's got a lot of wind to travel on, and it can stay dry, but not forever. Sooner or later, it's got to find a draw, some side canyon, where it can tuck down quick. That's when it starts to crack and thunder, but still keeps dry, working itself up into a dandy temper, ready to storm.

"Then it lets loose. Rains enough to set you afloat right where you're standing. It's scarifying. Bad enough if it runs hard by you, taking its head, but don't ever get yourself caught down a side canyon when a squall jumps over the rim. If you don't get whacked by lightning first, you're gonna go under. It

89

builds to a flash flood and comes at you like a wall. A live wall, with its tongue hanging out front of it.

"You watch that muddy tongue. It comes hissing at you, afore it laps up whatever it wants to get a lick at, and then lets the wall swallow. Gulps everything down its mud-choked throat, and what you see may look something like water, but it's coming for you like an avalanche.

"Crazy part is the rain's already gone. You're back to dry desert, but this dead lonesome wave is coming for you, rolling itself up into a mud ball, like one of them dirty comets you read about.

"Only it's got its dirty secret too. Hiding itself, just like a hermit. Outside the side canyon, less you're alert, and then some, you don't know it's coming. If you're down at the open end, you never maybe even heard the thunder, much less got rained on.

"What you hear is this rumble. I swear it is like the biggest semi you ever heard drive straight off a cliff, into the river.

"Around midmorning, it came out of Wriggleback, slamming into the Green, just above here, and rolled toward Flat Iron. It was rolling dead trees and rocks and boulders, this tremendous flood wave, but like it weren't doing nothing – Russ told me afterwards – but shooting marbles in a mud puddle."

The dog pawed at the air, but could gain no foothold.

She had jumped short, could feel herself falling, but in midair, still held her hinders tucked. At direst drop, she sprang them, kicking with all her broad back and both legs, flying at the emptiness. That gave her just enough thrust to pitch into the far tangle of the overhang, catch at a few straggling vines in its ripping web.

A splay-footed tumbler, clinging to a nearly missed net. From there, she had to risk the climb.

She worked awkwardly, biting at any fiber she could sink her teeth into, and pulled herself that last hitch over the rim by clamping her black jaw around a scrubby pine root, in a bleeding slaver of dirt.

She rose and rolled her brown eye back across the divide, and the old man raised his pipe one last time. In sweet warning, the pipe sang.

Rainwater at the foot of the canyon
Rainwater singing

She barked back at him once, twice. Still hesitating to leave him alone, stranded on the other tangled bluff.

But he waved her on, desperately, tearing at the mosses of his white hair.

Immediately she jumped away and stretched into her loping run, laying her black strength alongside the turbulence of the rumbling side canyon.

Water, hurtling down the long draw, kept up a brutal tumble of crest over rock, rock after surge, surge into crest. She could not match that elemental pace. But she was still game, and pulled on her large heart, her every sinew not to be outrun by this other roaring beast.

She could see its muddy tongue, out and slathering, just like her own.

That tongue flicked and probed, as the dirt-boiling wave rose, gathering into a boll, like a swollen hump. She was in a race to outrun that wave before its hump reached the river.

Once she stumbled. Her numb left hind paw caught in the crotch of a dead pinyon. That sent her sprawling some thirty feet like a tossed sack, but she was up again, allowing no quarter to the maverick flood.

She swerved into tighter thicket, nearer the mouth of the canyon, where the river was already swelling to a heaving, mud-choked bulge. Each surge stretched the taut, green surface, like a mossy drumhead.

Upriver, floating above this swell, she could see three rafts. They were growing fatter, so they had to be coming nearer. She fixed her blue eye on the flood danger, then turned her brown eye back toward the flotilla, swept up like torn lilypads, adrift toward the sizzling rapid.

Then she began to bark. Not howling, but still at full cry. She swung her muzzle high, set her four feet on that long axis of warning, and belled like a dog who has cornered the beast for her masters.

She kept barking, as she broke into a fast trot down river, to intercept them at the rapids.

Behind her, there rose a watery tattoo, beating to a rippling crescendo. Then the drumhead split open. Muddy tumescence burst into green insurgence, pushing the river high up the canyon walls. Flood waters drove a hissing lap line across the dark striations, in quickening measure of a lunging, hell-tide crest.

The lizard had hunched its sleek green back and raised up a dragon.

She ran through the snapping bottom foliage, shying back and forth to keep sight of the three rafts. They were soon caught by the hump of surging mud and thrashing trees and trolling uproar.

The boatmen fought desperately to keep their rafts headed. But the hump seized them athwart, twirled them round and round in its vicious flux, bending their long oars like jackstraws.

The dog was up on the Navajo sandstone when the first raft bellied into the swelling rapids.

It struck the geyser head on. The jet kicked the raft silly, and it nearly yawed over, but somehow made its battered escape. Only to be blindsided by the snarling lateral, which sent it circling down into the flume of the hole, like a merry-go-round cut free. The bald boatman whipped his oars like flails, but the raft went awash under the brutal wave and spewed out its load. The riders clung to the pillow ropes with white fists, and the bald boatman, on his knees, poled at the rocks, with one bladeless oar.

He had them barely out to safety when the second raft hit the geyser broadside and swept straight down the hole. Its rubbery shell, puckered by the suction, jammed between two deadly razor rocks. The girl in a porkpie hat had already lost an oar, could do nothing with the one remaining. Shooting water began to pour under the stuck raft, tilting it slowly upward, like a frypan.

Then a grey tree wreck came down, breaking apart on the rocks. Its snag-limbed trunk swung into the raft bottom with a sickening slap, tore a slash in the rubber, and tipped everything out of the frypan.

Screaming people and black cargo bobbed in the waves.

The dog kept barking, and jumping up and down on her forepaws, but held to her place.

Then the third raft rammed into the rapids, dragging a yellow kayak.

The geyser had taken wild, like a hard-heeled mule, kicking the raft into a slag of rocks, shattering both oars into shards. Then the lateral drove it spinning toward the hole. The blond boatman, oarless, reached

the body to a hitch in the rocks. She bit into the knot, tearing the blond hair, and marshalled all her strength against the downflow that pounded into the confounding hole.

She did not swim. She climbed.

She set her four feet on rock bottom and climbed out of the darkness, hauling her burden.

Her muzzle pushed into the flood, quickly found the down slope under the cascading current. She grappled up its slick, forcing her heft against the tonnage of the giant-humped river.

The body came to frantic life, weakly grabbed her fur. She felt its drag, but did not yield. She climbed smooth stone, then ragged rocks, clawing for any rough hold, until she was cut and bleeding, and a red foam stained the whitening rapids.

Then the frowning wave caught her again, drove her back down under. Near lost, she scrabbled until her muzzle found the vacuum in the gasping pall and roar of the hole, and broke through its seething grasp. Then she felt the body loose its grip on her shaggy fur, and they both plunged into roiling waves, out of the thrashing rocks.

Together they dragged themselves, both on all fours, into the swollen, murmuring shallows. She stayed at the blond boy's side, tracked him toward shore, nuzzled him when he faltered on his way.

Others came out to help him.

She shook herself, fluffing her shaggy fur dry again,

then trotted back upstream, straight into the rapids after any others not yet come ashore.

She helped pull out the white-haired man with the red eyes, and the girl who had lost her porkpie hat, and another man who wouldn't let go of a bent flute, and still another man who kept shaking water out of his curlicue horn, and another woman who was hanging and weeping and singing on the shoulder of the bald boatman.

Each of them stumbled or crawled or knelt down, safely ashore, and still the dog turned and swam back into the rapids.

Finally she came trucking ashore, guiding a stumbling man who stopped in the flood scatter at water's edge, dropped to his knees, and grabbed up a short shank of wood from all that flotsam.

Still on his knees, he put the shank to his lips, worked his stiff fingers, as if testing the wood, and tried to blow a few notes. They went sour.

When he tried again, a trill that was surely supposed to be sweet melody, they were worse. Sorrowful, plain nasty.

He turned the shank around, and found a split running up through the holes in the barrel, almost to the mouthpiece.

He got up off his knees, muttering, even swearing. Then turned angrily toward the river and, with a cry of disgust, equally foul and off key, hurled the cracked recorder out into the high waters.

The dog was off and running, the moment she saw it spinning in the air, whistling like any other stick.

She kept it well in sight on her sprint and jump into the river, was swimming hard when it splashed down, a tiny hit in all that upsurge, but dead in front of her. Forced by flood, but swimming with the current, she soon closed the distance. Its barrel floated half upright, and she snagged it, still sore-mouthed, and paddled back to shore.

Then trotted upstream, and out, and laid the stick at the astonished man's feet.

They cheered her hard, even gave in to fierce laughter, out of their own misery. She barked back at them, but that only made them cheer her on, send her off again, out into the river, after the wreckage of their music.

On one trip, she got all the way out to the weeping lady's cello, caught halfway up on a flat rock. It was womanly shaped, deeply in distress. She nudged its broad belly, and it gave shuddering thumps and thrums, but the river havoc was already breaking it apart. Shards and splinters washed away, leaving only its knobby scroll, like an abandoned clef.

Later, she swam far enough out to reach the harp. Broken loose from its big case, larking downstream until it lodged in a catch of driftwood. She climbed aboard, turning herself around and around on its delicate network of strings, as the river streamed through them, glissando.

One of her claws caught and plucked a string.

Its vibrations badly surprised her. She whirled around, much at a loss, plucking still more strings. Louder notes, until she stopped in her tracks, lowered her muzzle, nostrils quivering, to sniff.

She reached out a damping paw once, twice, then stepped slap hard on the dulcetly offending string, to stop its whining.

"I couldn't keep to sleep, and what was bothering me, that squall kept waking me up," Paul went on. "It was just riling itself when Jeff spotted it off the mesa, but headed who knew where to do what? It got into my head like one of those nightmares you keep waking up from but keep winding back to? Like a damn video. So I called Jeff early that Friday morning. Jeff said he hadn't heard nothing on the weather radio about where, or when or if, it come down. I said I wanted to go up before it had a chance to come down.

"We took off from the mesa, just after dawn, took us an hour to get over to Deso. By then it wasn't a squall anymore, only a mist trail off all the hot rock down to Wriggleback. And by the time we reached Wriggleback, it was a flash flood.

"You could see how it ran hard down that side draw. Like some critter bent on destruction. Cleaned that draw out like a gutter, then threw everything in the river.

"What we missed was that whole mess running through the rapids, and my party caught dead in front of the roll-out. All three rafts floated right into the peak of that flash flood, took Flat Iron at its crest. Jeff and I got there most a half hour later. The rapids were still boiling, but everything and everybody else was through, caught in the wash, or coming ashore. And damn glad they made it.

"So I heard the story from everybody but Blue Dog, and you can tell she's holding plenty back.

"You looked down, it was a sorry sight. The rafts were beached wherever they caught along the shore, really busted up, and we seen the Chamber Pots and Pam and Willie Bee pulling wet things out of the wash. What was left of their sorry little noisemakers. Russ was lying on the shore, flaked out, one arm flung over his eyes. The other arm is broke from sheer damn foolery, lucky to be alive, trying to shove rocks around in a rapid.

"But who is still out there in the rapids? Blue Dog. I spot her by damn, at long last, down there swimming around, kind of gingerly, then she pulls out, runs up the river shore, dives back in, to take another ride and poke around, see to it everybody's out.

"They are, and all that's left, near to hand, is that cello. Hung up on that flat-iron rock you see, way down there, behind the hole." Paul pointed out past the rooster tail, making things vivid. "You never seen anything more laughable sad. The Chamber Pots lost most all their instruments, that cello among them. Blue Dog did what she could. I say that cello would have drowned, if she didn't break up first, off that rock."

Paul had to have himself a chuckle on that. "Then Blue Dog took off downstream after that albino's harp. Harp got hung up too. You get Russ to tell you about how she got to play the last note.

"They were plenty hit by hardship, but happy enough they made it through. I can't really fault Russ, did as he was told. He took the last raft, tied on his yellow Dancer, and stood off to send Willie Bee and then Pam right on through.

"But once they were caught, he didn't see any way out. Says they were already past Wriggleback when the flood went for them. Like it was there waiting and some dam broke and out it roars. Russ says he yelled forward, 'Gang, we got to ride it out!' But it rolls straight under them, picked them up like those stump wrecks and whoosh! into those rocks. 'Like water running through a buzz saw,' Russ says. 'All set to saw you up into bite-sized pieces.'

"Russ was shook when Pam got jammed, and didn't quite keep his head. He figgered he could ram her loose, but that was damn folly. She panned over, and then he nearly jammed, and that landed him down the hole." Paul poked his red beard toward that whirlpool in Flat Iron. "Course it was considerable deeper, with the flood digging it out. 'A monster,' Russ tells me. He went sliding down, head first, scraping his knees, on what was... know what he says it was really like? *Like a sidewalk.* The damnedest thing. So he panicked, like some blind guy, grabbing his way through the rocks.

" 'But they are *smooth*,' he says. It's like he can't get up off *pavement*. The water is holding him down deep, pushing him under. Says he can't breathe. 'I'm upside down, surely drowning, but everywhere is flat, flat, flat.' He blacks out and makes this grab to claw at rock, concrete, anything. 'And I catch hold of fur.'

"He don't know where she comes from, but it's Blue. 'She got me up off the pavement.' He can feel her strength, pulling him up from flat-down drowning dead. 'She shouldered off the whole damn river to make me room.'

"That's how it must've been, but it also was the river. It took to flood something fierce, but even out of a bad frown, you can sometimes catch a forgiving wave. I believe that's what happened. The Green turned forgiving."

Paul finally rose off his spray skirt, dusted away the dirt, and said, "Only why did it? Time we made that run ourselves." We dropped down the embankment, back toward our beached kayaks. He used the walk for the last bit of story he had left.   .

"What puzzles me is Blue Dog. How come she took so sudden to the wild, then came right back home again? I can see how Marv Carter's party did their part with that Denver desperado setting up his own free-fire zone. But that ain't enough to explain Blue Dog. She was maybe scared off, but I swear she also hankered off.

"Now is that the old chicken thief in her? A chicken thief born or raised to have a wild streak? I figgered

I had her trained back to law-abiding, but if that training don't take 'less I'm around to see it does, what's it worth? Or is it instinct that sent her hankering off? Whatever that means.

"You can see she's part some kind of shepherd and part Lab and some Newfy or even bloodhound, but I swear there's more to her mix than that. So is it some border collie gone renegade inside her? Some long time back, was Blue Dog bred up ready to set off on her own whenever some wilderness calls?"

We were down beside our kayaks, ready to launch into the calm, flat-rolling current of the Green.

"Russ never did see his yellow Dancer again. It took off like that cello," Paul got sidetracked. "But I figger those are blunt objects. Current can do what it wants with them. Take them off into the wild, who's to know?

"But can't be that way with Blue Dog. If she went off into the wild, she come back because something in the wild sent her back. Fact is, sent her back to do what she is supposed to do. To do what I'd trained her up to do. She's a raft dog, and I still say she come back and done right, out of whatever crossbreeding she had for a fair start, and despite all the bad tricks she ever learned.

"Now where does that leave her?" We were set to shove off, slip out the nearest eddy gate into the green rush of the river. "I'll tell you where. She's got to've been in other hands. Other hands that are just as savvy and gripping as mine, no matter what ways whoever it is may follow. If it's the ways of the wilderness, maybe a touch more deft than I am."

He picked up his paddle in one hand, overhead, and gave it a fluttering spin-and-twirl with consummate skill.

"What I'm saying is, I'm sharing Blue Dog. I know I am, but who with? A dog can't serve two masters, but can you say that if the masters never meet? What if one of them, the wild one, the secret one, sometimes alters for the other one? What if both of them run the same dog, up and down this river, so she can really, truly serve her own nature?"

Paul pushed off the bank, and tucked his blade into the eddy.

"I leave you with that for a thought. And I say it's one damn good reason why there might still be some of the Old People around. Ain't I showed you their picture?"

We paddled for the rapids, and I cut into the mainstream V behind Paul's red stern, wagging at me like a stump tail. The arrow narrowed, curled into a misting jet through the first rocks, almost on top of the rooster tail. I caught its wet feathering, cut river left to escape the lateral that pressed me hard toward the hole. Paul deliberately sashayed right over all this frowning froth, but I gave its ugly depths a wide berth.

A fast current headed us smoothly toward Nefertiti, where Paul planned to pull out. He turned once into another eddy to point out a high slit in the loftiest cliff that had to be an ancient kiva, he assured me. "Might still be living there." I said I doubted that, after more than a thousand years. "You ever been up there?" he grinned, pointing with his paddle, beyond the range of possibility. "How can you be sure?"

He stroked out of the gate, back into the green rush, paddling at an easy pace, to stay with the current. The river sank swiftly down its great rock trough, and we passed the other spot where John Wesley Powell might have gotten himself cliffed, then rescued by his companion's long johns. "Could have used a good hound dog on that trip," Paul shouted back at me.

Then we were around a far bend, up against the freak rock profile of the Egyptian queen, complete with her regal hat, a granite outcropping that crowned her utterly detailed rock face. When I looked, it was amazing. She stared right back at you, askance, from that socket with the missing eye.

"She's older than the Old People," he said, "only because she is rock."

Ashore, I heard barking, and Paul shouted, "Blue Dog! Blue!"

There she was, a big, loping animal, with shaggy black fur in a nap of curls. I caught her two-color eyes, a tad wonky in her large head, but what struck me, either eye, is how alert she looked at you. Already smart to how you might act. She trotted back and forth, back and forth at Paul's hail, splashing the foam curl. She was all frisky welcome, until her hunter's muzzle rose,

sniffing the air, and she shifted her big Lab paws, ever so delicately to stock still.

"Want you to see this!" Paul whispered hoarsely, and waved me to stay put in my kayak.

She kept her black poise, but the muzzle slowly lowered, and her neck stretched out to form a single ridge line with her stiffening tail.

"Watch," Paul barely mouthed.

And she lifted her right paw, slowly bending the fore leg, steady as a rock.

Out of the tamarisk thicket, two chukar came flapping, breasting the air in a brace that was the nearest thing to game birds I'd ever seen burst out of any desert river break.

"She can hold point!" Paul shouted, in giddy celebration. "Now you tell me where *that* come from!"

A NOTE ON THE TEXT

The Native American poems quoted in *Blue Dog, Green River* are taken from "19th-Century Versions of American Indian Poetry" in *American Poetry: The Nineteenth Century*, volume two, edited by John Hollander and published by the Library of America.

A NOTE ON THE TYPE

Blue Dog, Green River has been set in Monotype Ehrhardt. An offshoot of Stanley Morison's researches into the so-called Janson faces, Ehrhardt was based on types cut during the late sixteenth century by the Hungarian punchcutter Nicholas Kis (1650–1702) for the Ehrhardt foundry in Leipzig. A clergyman, Kis traveled to Holland to study printing and punchcutting in hopes of broadening his experience of the world. His success as a punchcutter was considerable – his fame reached as far as the court of Cosimo II de' Medici – but he chose to return to his homeland, where he hoped to print beautiful bibles. This venture ended in frustration, but the types were widely popular. ✧ In later years, Kis's work was perennially misattributed to Anton Janson; even D. B. Updike – who set his *opera magna*, *The Book of Common Prayer*, in Janson – failed to connect Kis's name to the types in his massive *Printing Types*. Morison's research revealed that Janson was not the author of the types, but it remained for Harry Carter and George Buday to correct the attribution and give Kis his due.

Design & composition by Carl W. Scarbrough